Put Yourself in My Shoes
Somos8 Series

© Text: Susanna Isern, 2020
© Illustrations: Mylène Rigaudie, 2020
© Edition: NubeOcho, 2020
© Translation: Ben Dawlatly, 2020
www.nubeocho.com · hello@nubeocho.com

Original title: *Ponte en mi lugar*
Text editing: Laura Victoria Fielden,
Cecilia Ross and Rebecca Packard

First edition: 2020
ISBN: 978-84-17673-37-6
Legal Deposit: M-19648-2019

Printed in Portugal.

Put Yourself in My Shoes

Susanna Isern   Mylène Rigaudie

nubeOCHO

Spring had finally arrived. It was
a beautiful day, and Cricket decided
to go for a stroll. After the long winter,
he was eager to see his friends.

Ladybug, Cricket's neighbor, was searching for something amongst the stones in her garden.

"What are you looking for, Ladybug?" asked Cricket.

"Oh, it's terrible! I hung my spots out to dry, and now I can't find one of them."

"I don't wear any spots. I don't think they're that important."

Ladybug carried on searching, and Cricket went back to his walk.

He came across Bee sitting next to her hive.

"What's up, Bee?" asked Cricket.
"Some fishing twine got tangled around one of my wings, and now I can't fly."

"I hardly ever use my wings. I don't think they're that important."
Bee kept on trying to untangle herself, and Cricket went on his way.

Later on, he bumped into Spider, who was making silk.

"Why are you in such a rush, Spider?"
"I'm running low on balls of silk. I need to stock up before I open the store."

"I never buy balls of silk. I don't think they're that important."
Spider kept on working, and Cricket headed toward the river.

Centipede was very busy sewing shoes near the riverbank.

"How come you're working so hard, Centipede?"

"I need to make a hundred shoes so I can go for a walk."
"Well, I never use shoes. I don't think they're that important."

Centipede went back to sewing, and Cricket left
the riverbank and continued walking.

While Cricket was enjoying his stroll, Ladybug ran into Bee and helped her untangle her wing.

After that, Bee and Ladybug noticed that Spider had a lot of work to do, so they helped him wind his silk.

Later on, Bee, Ladybug and Spider went to
help Centipede sew his one hundred shoes.

Then they all went looking for Ladybug's
missing spot, which had gotten caught on
a high branch.

It was starting to get dark, and it was time to go home. Cricket could not stop thinking about how strange his friends had been acting all day.

Once home, Cricket put on his suit and bow tie and
grabbed his violin. He loved playing at nightfall!

Cricket took a deep breath, picked up the bow, and started to draw it across the violin strings. But before any music could be heard...

TWANG!

The violin strings, which had rusted over the winter, snapped.

Cricket searched desperately all over his house for some new strings, but he couldn't find any.

Just then, Flea appeared at his window.

"What are you looking for, Cricket?"
"My violin strings have broken. I need some new ones."
"I don't play the violin. I don't think it's that important."

"What do you mean it's not important?
Put yourself in my shoes, Flea!" Cricket shouted
angrily as Flea went out the door.

Cricket suddenly thought of his friends. Perhaps Ladybug's spots, Bee's wing, Spider's balls of silk, and Centipede's shoes were important after all. He hadn't put himself in their shoes.

Cricket hurried out. He needed to apologize to his friends.

He had barely opened the door when he saw them all standing right outside his house.

"But... what are you all doing here?" Cricket said.

"We came over because we thought it was odd that we couldn't hear your violin on such a nice spring evening," explained Ladybug.
"We suspected there might be a problem with your strings," added Spider.
"So we brought you these..." said Centipede.

Cricket was touched. He removed the broken strings from his violin and attached a length of Ladybug's clothesline, the fishing twine that had gotten tangled around Bee's wing, a piece of silk from Spider, and a shoestring from one of Centipede's shoes.

That night, under the moonlight, Cricket played the liveliest song in his repertoire. Ladybug, Bee, Spider and Centipede skipped and danced all night long. Even Flea came back to join the party.

Cricket looked up at the starry night sky as he played his instrument. That night he felt very special, because now his music sounded like Ladybug and her clothesline, Bee and her fishing twine, Spider and his ball of silk, and Centipede and his shoestring.